# UNIFIED SECRETS, INC.

## A SHORT SCIENCE FICTION STORY

### SUPER GREAT CHALLENGE STORIES
### BOOK 9

## RYAN M. WILLIAMS

Unified Secrets, Inc. © 2025 Ryan M. Williams
Cover art © 2025 Ryan M. Williams
Cover design by Ryan M. Williams

All Rights Reserved

No part of this book may be reproduced in any form or by any electronic or mechanical means including information storage and retrieval systems, without permission in writing from the author. The only exception is by a reviewer, who may quote short excerpts in a review.

This book is a work of fiction. Names, characters, places, and incidents either are products of the author's imagination or are used fictitiously. Any resemblance to actual persons, living or dead, events, or locales is entirely coincidental.

Visit our website at ryanmwilliams.com

Glittering Throng Press

PO BOX 179

RAINIER WA 98576-0179

eBook ISBN-13: 978-1-946440-94-5

Paperback ISBN-13: 978-1-946440-95-2

GTP NO. 51
SGC NO. 09

# ACKNOWLEDGMENTS

This story is one of 52 weekly stories written (and published) over a year. It's part of the Super Great Challenge (SGC) run by Dean Wesley Smith and Kristine Kathryn Rusch through the WMG Publishing workshops on Teachable. Without that challenge, this story (and the others) likely wouldn't exist.

Additionally, in creating the cover art for the stories in the SGC, I've typically used Blender—my **favorite application ever**—an open source, free, 3D modeling, digital painting, animation, sculpting, and video editing application. I've taken courses and watched tutorials from creators like Ducky 3D, SouthernShotty, Grant Abbitt, Curtis Holt, the Blender Studio, CG Cookie, CG Boost, the Blender Guru and so many others. It's a wonderful and inspiring community.

And I'm so grateful for the **sup-**

**port of my members** on my site (ryanmwilliams.com) for their encouragement for this challenge. My family has also been instrumental in making this possible. It helps immensely having people behind me on this journey. Thank you.

———

# CHAPTER 1

# FROM NASA'S KENNEDY SPACE CENTER

---

*...reports of hacking of the new Ares Mars Orbiter (AMO), stating that the latest high-resolution images of the Mars surface haven't been tampered with or modified. Initial reports suggested that the large letters that appeared mysteriously on the face of Mons Olympus were a hoax. Now, with confirmation from the Chinese and SpaceX satellites, the administration states that images accurately reflect the reality—within the past month, some agency has constructed an enormous 1,000-*

*meter long sign in tall capital letters, reading, "Humans, Fuck Off." And on the other side of the planet, in Hellas Planitia, another sign reading "Hands-Off Mars." The administration has made no comment regarding who might have pulled off this act of what some call interplanetary graffiti.*

---

CHORTLING, Auggy Perch, real name August Perch, kicked a slippered foot against the concrete floor to spin his ergonomic chair around. He was treated to a dizzying picture of the pale orange basement walls, OLED lights glowing with a soft blue through the translucent trim around the ceiling. Shelves featuring his collection of props, books, and toys spun past. It was a familiar blur. He stopped his motion when he came back around to face his computers again. He leaned back, picking up his insulated thermos and sucking flat water from the straw, while admiring his screens. It was a great setup, like something out of a science fiction movie—four large curved monitors, two in front of him, two above, and two more in profile mode on each side of the cluster. All of it mounted in a custom frame he had printed. It created a huge bubble expanse of screen real estate—his canvas for his creations. The entire bubble was mounted on an armature from the ceiling, making it easy to reposition, raise, lower, and rotate. He could move between his office chair, to standing, to reclining in his hammock, and bring the sphere where he wanted.

He flipped between browser tabs, looking at the news stories on one window. Another mirrored his phone, showing the ongoing Tik Tok posts as people weighed in. Other screens showed feeds from Instagram, Blue Sky, Reddit, and many others. Plus a screen with Marie's Instagram feed, mostly pictures of Cicy. His own programs scouring the content online, compiling, and summarizing it for him. He chuckled, scrolling past conspiracy theorists, science buffs, and reactors alike. He picked up plain popcorn from a 3d printed skull bowl and popped it in his mouth, crunching as he read what the world was saying.

*Hoax,* was a common thread. Distrust in the government to report the truth wasn't dented much by the confirmation from other agencies. Even the uneducated public knew that what they were seeing on Mars couldn't possibly be real. No country, no commercial effort, could have sent people to Mars to construct the signs on the planet. For proof, they argued that there were no pictures of the signs being constructed. The timeline was narrowed by the satellite orbits. Nothing there on one pass, the sign visible in the next.

*Of course not.* He had accounted for the orbits of every satellite around Mars, specifically to avoid being seen putting up the signs. He chuckled again to himself. The evidence was undeniable—but flat earthers existed, so no telling how stupid people could get. He'd given them definitive proof that their entire reality had shifted and they cried hoax. The *experts* scrambled, trying to find an explanation that would keep their reality intact, while acknowledging the "apparent reality" of the signs on Mars.

It was all good fun, even if the purpose was serious. He chuckled again, pushed back from the desk, and stood, turning around to admire his greatest creation—the greatest invention in human history. It set off butterflies in his stomach. Auggy slid his hands into his blue jean pockets.

Any science fiction fan would recognize it immediately. They might get the details wrong, but they'd get the idea from the design. Similar objects existed in so many books, shows, and movies. Some had been depicted as an arch, signifying a passage. Others a sort of booth or pad. Something that you stood on, or in, usually with all sorts of technological grebbles around it. Many of the devices also had a sort of control console in front of it, though not all utilized that feature. They all had one thing in common—they were impossible. A story-telling device to move people and things from one scene to another without the whole messy business of vehicles. Or sometimes vehicles also went through the device, because they'd be useful at the destination. It moved the reader or viewer to the next scene without the whole boring process of watching people travel. If the travel was an important part of the story, then the writers would find a reason to make the device temporarily unusable.

Auggy rocked on his bare feet. He flexed muscled, fit arms, t-shirt tightening across broad shoulders. A little sore from all the work he'd been doing, but it wasn't bad. He'd get in a work out, maybe a run before it got dark. It'd be good to get out of the basement and out on the trails. He loved running through the woods at dusk, air cooling, on up to the ridge where he could watch the sun set and imagine that he could travel back in time and see the familiar landscape transformed into a world that hadn't known the axes and saws that made a farm out of an ecosystem. For the moment, though, he took pleasure in *looking* at his invention.

He'd gone with a pod design. It wasn't strictly necessary, except that he wanted an airlock. It made the whole process both easier and harder. It was a sleek, shiny white pod made from various panels and then painted and covered in a clear gloss. It matched the esthetic of his monitor bubble. The process for making both shells was the same. The design took a lot from old science fiction, more Kubrick than Scott. The hatch at the front had a large window to the interior so he could set up the tripod in the room and film himself entering the pod. He believed in keeping meticulous records. He'd made a lot of things over the years. There were the patented inventions, the ones he was willing to release, that gave him the money to pursue whatever he wanted. Then he had shared more personal projects, often inspired by fandom. Props, cosplay, and the like, his videos building him a large online following in those circles. Mostly the props were simply for fun, because they were cool and he liked making things.

*You've got too much stuff,* Marie had said one time, back before she left.

And then there were the inventions and insights that he didn't share with anyone. Auggy walked closer to the pod, eyes scanning over its surface for any imperfections. He approached it with the same appreciation and love that other men gave to restored classic cars. He thought he might redo some of the panel latches. Right now they stood up slightly from the panels' surfaces. He could hide them beneath a pressure release switch instead. The latches did look good on video, though.

*It wasn't that important.* He grinned. The pod worked. Everything now was only refining it. Especially the suit. *Although that wasn't even the main point, was it?*

He touched the panel beside the hatch, activating it to scan his fingerprints and pulse. Embedded cameras at the corners of the hatch used facial recognition, matching his pulse visible through capillary action in his face with the reading from his finger, while breath analyzers picked up his exhalations for any stress molecules or foreign chemicals. *Complete overkill, but it was cool.* None of the security would prevent someone from breaking in if they wanted to—but why would they? No one had any reason to suspect this was anything except an elaborate prop he'd built. In his videos, he called it a prop, a hang-out space, and a set for future videos.

The hatch moved in and slid to the side with a really cool *whoosh*. Auggy strolled inside, into the small outer chamber. The space that looked like it was the entire interior of the pod. The only space that he showed on his videos. It was set up with another hammock on one side of the room. Screens set in the wall made it a great place to hang out and game. The main floor area was clear and large enough for him to play VR games and workouts. A window beside the hammock—that should have shown the rest of the basement—instead showed a bright lunar landscape outside. Those watching his videos thought it was a special effect, what with the Apollo 17 lander sitting out there in the distance. A high-resolution monitor behind the window frame, synced to the camera to provide parallax perspective. *Because that's what he told them it was.* He'd even done the build to *make* that window. Only it wasn't the window in place now. His window showed the truth—the surface of the Moon. The other window had already been recycled for other parts.

The window showed the truth of the pod and no one realized. He loved that.

TEN YEARS. *It'd taken that long.* Auggy crossed the antechamber to the left, out of view of a camera outside (if he had one set up). This was where he set up the camera and lights when filming himself on the other side of the pod, with the hammock and lunar window in the background. Which meant his followers never saw this side of the pod. From the exterior shots, there wasn't much on that side since it was pretty much up against the basement wall. It'd taken him ten years to get to this point. Really, a blink of the eye to go from theory to practical applications. There was a double door in front of him, bright orange, smooth, and a panel on the short wall beside it. Except he didn't need to do anything with the panel. The doors slid apart of their own accord, also with the same cool "whoosh" sound.

The space beyond the doors was a wide hexagonal room with a domed ceiling. Equipment occupied the spaces around the room. Computers, control areas, pipes and conduits that led out into other sections. At the center of the room was a platform raised up from the floor. *Not ADA compliant.* It looked cool. The surface was a glittering resin composite with a clear central area. A large ring light hung from the overhead dome over the platform. As Auggy moved to the right, a rectangular sort of *doorway* became visible. It had no thickness, couldn't be seen edge on. But when he walked around, he was looking through a rectangular opening in the air that started at the platform, was seven feet high and forty-two inches wide. It looked *exactly* like looking through a regular open door, only this one showed the red and rocky Martian landscape outside.

Ten years, and he had created the science that allowed him to alter the spacetime coordinates in a specific area —rewriting the fabric of space itself to connect one location to another location in the universe. A secret he hadn't shared with *anyone*, not even Marie. It might not have made a difference, he didn't know. Probably not. The double doors he'd passed through to enter the lab and the lunar window in the antechamber were both the same sort of fields. The equipment maintained the fields, drawing on his power core, which used (*in basic terms*) the inflation of the universe itself to power everything.

He crossed the lab and dropped into a waiting chair, the twin of the one back in his basement. The lab existed a mile beneath his house. The same technology used to generate the spacetime coordinate field, gave him the ability to manipulate the field to easily move matter from one place to another. He controlled the field parameters, allowing only what he wanted to pass through the field. He used it to cut this chamber deep into the Earth. No need to worry about pressure or heat—the field kept all of that at bay. Air circulated from the surface. The Martian doorway on the platform showed a typical dull day on the red planet. His sign in Hellas Planitia, "Hands Off Mars," stood bright in contrast to the red-hued surface. Already, though, he could see the dust clinging to the fabric letters. Each was simple, an expanding aluminum frame with a white polymer fabric. He'd tilted them back to make them more visible to the satellites when they passed over. Eventually the wind, the sand, and the radiation would break apart the polymer. The letters would turn to tatters, break down, and be dispersed across a region of the red planet.

It contaminated the planet. More human trash on what was an *almost* untouched world. He appreciated the care that scientists and researchers took in their missions to explore. He understood the desire, the passion to learn, but it didn't stop there. Instead there were billionaires determined to not only put humans (*and the entire support infrastructure necessary to keep humans alive*) on Mars, but to exploit the resources of the planet. Whether or not life had ever developed on Mars was beside the point. *Why couldn't people look at something without wanting to mess it up?*

Auggy leaned forward, elbows on his knees, and gazed out at the Martian landscape. *He*, August Perch, had been the first human to walk on the surface of another planet. He swiveled slightly. Across the room, in a suspension frame, hung his spacesuit. It wasn't an independent suit. Lines plugged into the back of the suit, feeding it air, water, and power. Everything he needed to stay alive. He could put it on and walk through that doorway onto Mars, dragging his lines behind him (*he had encased them in durable carbon fiber reinforced sleeves*). They didn't have to go far. He programmed the doorway to move with him, tracking him so it was always a step behind. At any moment he could step back and be in the lab. In an medical emergency the safety line would automatically retract and pull him back to the lab. It hadn't taken him long to put up the signs. He pushed the letters through, stepped over, and went down the line, standing them up for each word.

Walking on another world was... *weird*.

And scary.

# CHAPTER 3

# TAKING A WALK

UP until the moment when Auggy was about to step through his doorway to Mars, an irrational part of his brain was afraid. The doorway was stable. He had already taken samples through the doorway. The sign letters were tumbled out there onto the sands of Mars. He'd built the lab and had used the doorway to visit all sorts of places on Earth.

But this was his first off-world trip. Part of his brain kept insisting that he couldn't be sure of the impact it would have on him, despite all of the testing. Mars was nearly 128 million miles away, currently. His doorway erased distances, literally connecting different spacetime coordinates to create a doorway. He could manipulate the interface, allowing visible light through, but filtering out radiation. He could keep the air molecules from rushing through to the thin atmosphere on the other side —while allowing air molecules in his body and suit to pass unhindered. It kept sand and dust from Mars on that side of the barrier. The interface screened anything he wanted, or conversely, could be used like a one-way screen. It could pass through matter, leaving everything as it was, while extracting particular elements. He had extracted gold from old gold mines that way, creating an extra fund for when he needed it. The same technique hollowed out the lab and kept it intact. The field at the door connected to his basement, within the pod. The original doorway generator was in the pod, that he had used to create the lab and develop the technology. It still created the window to the Apollo 17 landing site on the Moon.

Auggy's breath sounded harsh in his helmet. At least to his ears. The moment should be memorialized, somehow. He wished he had Marie here to tell him if he he said the wrong thing. It was historic, even though he'd known it would work. The first human to walk on another planet. It should have been out of reach, even for someone with his intellect. But it was real. He was really standing in front of an open door to another world. It seemed like the time to say something. He looked up where the suit camera was filming him.

"After everything that humans have done to Earth, why can't we leave the rest of the solar system alone? Research is one thing. Exploitation is another." He grinned. "Why don't we fuck off?"

*It's what she said, telling him to fuck off.*

Pushing aside the thought, he stepped through the doorway. Stepping from the basement to the lab wasn't noticeable. It felt like walking from one room to another. The interface was undetectable unless it showed something out of place, or you could see it disappear by looking at the edge—*lack of an edge.* This time his foot didn't come down as fast as expected. It was like moving in slow motion. A delay and then his boot crunched down on the rocks and dust. The other step followed. The light changed, dimmed in his perspective.

*I'm on Mars.* He cleared his throat. "I'm on Mars. I'm the first human to set foot on this planet—and I hope I'm the last. Let's put up the sign."

*Not bad. It was too the point.*

It took thirty minutes of work, shuffling across the gentle slope of Olympus Mons—it was so large, the largest volcano in the solar system, that he couldn't really tell it was a mountain. The letters stood up at the angle to make them visible to the satellites, the bases anchored in place with rocks.

Finished, Auggy took a final look and stepped backwards. His full weight returned and he braced himself, feeling for a moment that he had suddenly shouldered a heavy burden. Air jets fired and vacuums in the platform activated, blowing Martian dust from his suit. It roared against him from every direction and above. The jets moved, high-resolution cameras scanning for any trace of the red dust on the white suit fabric. The process took fifteen minutes before the system shut off.

"I guess I'm clean now," Auggy said. He shuffled over to the suit rack to get out of it.

That'd been the first time. He'd done Hellas Planitia two days later.

# ONLINE COMMENTS

Obvs a hoax, altered footage, or AI.

SpaceX did it. Pedos trafficking girls to Mars.

No way set up by robots if so where are they? Had to be people.

Fake, god u r so stupid

What's next?

# FROM KENNEDY SPACE CENTER...

---

*The sudden loss of communication from the various missions to Mars was apparently resolved today with the sudden appearance of the robotic explorers and orbiters here at Kennedy Space Center. Every robotic explorer from Perseverance and Curiosity, to the Mars orbiters, to the original Viking landers were discovered this morning outside the Kennedy Space Center, all lined up in the order they were sent to the Red Planet. We've also received reports that missions sent by other countries have also reappeared back on Earth. This follows the messages that appeared on Mars apparently telling humans to leave Mars alone.*

---

AUGGY SIPPED his tea and watched the news reports and social feeds on the screens in his lab deep beneath the Earth's surface. The arguments about the signs being a hoax had shifted now with concrete proof of a power people didn't understand. The scientists would be thrilled to receive all of the samples that Perseverance had stored away, abandoned for years after the return missions were scrapped. A parting gift to science. Everyone else was scared and confused.

He leaned back in the chair. It'd been an easy bit of programming to have the doorway sweep up each of the missions and deposit them at their respective agencies. It'd keep people busy for a long time. He'd also used the doorway pick up the signs he had planted and brought those back to drop into the mantle, melting to nothing.

The tracks from rovers and his footprints would disappear in time with the action of wind on Mars.

He couldn't help but wonder how this would shift the conversations on Earth. Already there were many calls for new missions to be launched to Mars to uncover who—or what—was behind the 'pranks'. Saner voices pointed out that the power behind these so-called pranks could probably return any mission as easily. The fear was also increasing. The more paranoid voices asked what else could be done by this power?

*Good question.*

Auggy had plenty of ideas. Too many ideas. The doorway gave him essentially unlimited power. He could have anything he wanted. He could remove all of the nuclear waste, weapons, toxic spills—any of it. Using the doorway, he could clean up the planet. With his control over the interface he could end wars. He could transfer food and water to people in starving countries. That didn't even begin to touch the other uses of the interface. He'd already begun exploring the medical applications. The interface could act as the perfect medical imagining and treatment device. Step through the doorway and have it programmed to remove any cancerous or pre-cancerous cells, trim down the number of fat cells, and eliminate any dangerous viruses, phages, or bacteria. He had work to do on that use, but that was only details. It could do so much more. Repair genetic damage. Erase physical wounds. Not by himself, though. He'd need help. People with medical training along with other people that could be trained to understand how to program and control the interface. That meant even more people.

Then, thinking even bigger, ecosystem restoration. Scrubbing excess carbon dioxide and methane from the atmosphere—that was an easier one, the doorway could filter those molecules, transferring them directly into the Earth's mantel. He could pull trash and pollutants from the ocean and fresh water supplies.

Auggy shook his head. *It's too*

*much.* How could he figure it all out on his own? It was daunting.

To do everything, he'd need to create more power generators, more equipment, computing power, and many, many more people. And once he started, where would it stop? He could replace every transportation method in the world with simple doorways. No need for cars, trains, ships, or planes. His power generator could provide endless free and clean energy. No resource limitations and no destruction of the natural environment. Given that, then the world economic systems would unravel, become unnecessary. The programmable nature of the doorway interface meant it could gather resources and deposit them exactly like anything else that had passed through the interface—making it able to perfectly duplicate anything.

Auggy kicked a foot against the floor, rotating the chair.

*If he could do all of that, didn't he have an obligation to do it?*

It wasn't what he'd wanted when he started. It was a neat idea that became a theory, then an engineering and development problem. Like a flower, the possibilities had opened up before him. Each led to the next, more and more, revealing all the ways that science fiction had been short-sighted when it showed similar technology.

The interface granted him control of spacetime.

*Power of a god.* He didn't believe in gods, but this must be what it was like. He spun the chair around, tablet on his lap, and opened the interface.

The doorway appeared above the platform at the center of the lab. The other side was the lunar surface, looking toward the Apollo 17 landing site, just like his window 'upstairs' in his basement. The interface was tuned to only allow visible light through from the lunar side, filtered, but pure sunlight poured out onto the platform. Nothing from the lab passed through to the other side. If someone was on the Moon they wouldn't see anything. No doorway. It was the ultimate one-way mirror.

Auggy tapped a pre-programmed shortcut.

THE VIEW through the doorway changed. It showed an apartment living room. The mode allowed light from the apartment to pass through. It transmitted molecular vibrations, allowing sound to pass through into the lab. Nothing from his side passed through, meaning the doorway didn't exist on the other end. It couldn't be entered or detected. Guilt tugged at him, but he didn't switch the view.

The apartment was tastefully, if frugally, decorated. A small living room furnished with a orange corduroy coach with three seats and puffy cushions that somehow looked chic. It faced a large, flat, wall-mounted screen. An acrylic coffee table with sides that curved beneath to form legs sat in front of the couch. A wood rocking chair with bright blue cushions sat to one side near the interface. A painting of a seascape hung on the wall above the couch, waves foaming in a storm, but a shaft of sunlight shone through upon the graceful form of a leaping dolphin. The only occupant in the room was a calico cat that blended somewhat into the couch where it was curled up. *Cicy.*

Auggy reached to reset the interface. Marie walked out of the hallway into the living room. His hand froze above the screen, finger shaking above the button as he guiltily drank in the site of her. She was dressed in faded blue jeans, strategically torn across the thighs, widening out almost to a bell bottom at the foot. Her feet were bare, smooth soft brown, with nails painted a soft blue. She wore a white knit-cotton crop top, sleeveless, and her belly button piercing glittered. Her dark hair floated around her head like a soft aura. Her face was round, showing some of her father's Japanese ancestry, but mostly she took after her mother. She held her phone in her hand, flicking the screen with her thumb to scroll.

*It's wrong to spy on her.* He reached over to the movement controls and used them to pass through the wall into the apartment's open hallway, turning to face her door. Before he could question it, he stood up, and grabbed his doorway fob from the charging pad on a pedestal near the platform. He stepped up onto the platform and strode through the doorway into the apartment's hallway. A breeze blew through from the open sides at either end where the stairwells climbed to each floor. The door in front of him was painted a dark blue, the silver numbers 380 attached above the peephole. It also had a camera doorbell beside the door.

He pressed the key fob button that basically collapsed the interface down to the width of an atom, keeping it centered in the fob. It'd maintain communication links with his system. When he wanted to go back, he could press the other button and step back through the invisible doorway. It was quite the vanishing trick.

He pocketed the fob, rubbed his

hands against his pants, then reached over and pressed the doorbell button.

"Auggy?"

"Hey, Marie. If you wouldn't mind, I could use someone to talk to."

His heart hammered with each passing second. He waited, trying not to look too anxious, knowing she was able to see him through the app on her phone.

Then he heard the welcome sound of the deadbolt turning. She opened the door partway, glancing over her shoulder, then back to him. "Get in before Cicy makes a dash for it."

Well aware of the cat's quick escape attempts, Auggy turned sideways, stepping through the opening as Marie moved out of his way. She pushed the door closed and then walked away, back into the meeting room. She turned back around when she was beside the coffee table, crossing her arms, head tilted slightly as she gave him a puzzled expression.

"What's going on Auggy? You wanted to talk? What about?"

He took a couple steps closer, then stopped. He rubbed his hands together.

*Telling Marie, it was a risk. But he'd kept the secret and it pushed them apart.*

"I'm ready to tell you." At her blank look, he said, "About my project."

Understanding showed in her face, then she frowned. "Auggy, have you been out of touch? Haven't you seen the news?"

It was his turn to not understand. "News?"

She held up her phone, screen facing him. The orbital picture with the words "Humans Fuck Off" was displayed. "The signs on Mars? Then this morning all of the missions appeared back here, no Earth. Even little Sojourner, the Viking landers—everything is back. Ingenuity. And their discards, all of the parachutes, lander shells, bits and pieces. It's all back. I think that's a bit more urgent than whatever you didn't want to share about your YouTube channel."

Confusion blossomed across her face as Auggy began laughing.

# CHAPTER 7

# MISTAKES

LAUGHING HADN'T BEEN his intent. As Marie's expression turned from confusion to something darker, Auggy held up his hands. He got control over himself with a few deep breaths.

"Sorry. I'm sorry, Marie. I didn't mean to laugh. That's actually what I meant. I wanted to talk to you about it."

"What does that have to do with your top secret project?"

Auggy didn't say anything. He folded his hands together in front of himself and tried hard not to grin like an idiot.

Marie opened her mouth. Closed it. Looked at the phone. At him.

"You're..."

Auggy nodded.

Marie stared at him for several seconds. Then she shook her head. "There's no way, Auggy. I don't know what you thought you were doing, coming over here with this story. It isn't funny."

He'd expected that. *Why should anyone believe him?* He could do things that people thought were impossible. It hadn't even been about trust. He trusted Marie. How could he tell her that he had solved the unified theory? She was an astronomer, not a physicist, but she had a good understanding of relativity and quantum mechanics.

He took out the doorway fob. "Let me demonstrate. It'll be easier."

Her eyes narrowed. "What's that?"

"A key, nothing more," he said, smiling. "And if I turn it this way—"

He pressed the fob button that reengaged the interface. Then he pressed the third button, the one that made the doorway visible and fixed the position.

Marie's sharp intake of breath and widening eyes was a mild reaction, really. She handled it very well.

Auggy stepped to the side and

turned so the doorway was to his right and Marie to his left. The doorway matched the floor and rose up above his head. It was wide and the visibility setting allowed light to cross both ways so it looked—*was*—a clear opening into the lab. He was pretty happy how cool the lab looked. He extended his hand through the interface, showing it was possible.

"Can I show you my lab?" he said.

Marie cleared her throat and pointed. "That's a portal."

"Pretty much," he agreed. "More than a simple portal. I have a lot of control over the interface."

She looked at his face, eyes searching. He smiled gently. She looked back at the doorway.

"What's that place? It isn't your basement."

"It's my sub-basement," he said. "I used the interface to create a pocket a mile beneath my house."

She made a small squeaking noise. "A mile?"

He shrugged. "I wanted a secure location. There's no connection to the surface, except through the interface.

Power generation happens on site at the lab."

"Geothermal?" she said, her voice faint.

Auggy shook his head. "Spacetime inflation."

She looked at him, eyes wide, and mouthed the words. She drew herself up and looked at him properly. "August Perch, what the hell are you doing?"

"I need help, Marie. I need *you*. Your help working out what to do next."

"You shouldn't have started by pulling pranks like those signs! People think either some country has advanced tech, or its aliens. I was going for the alien theory, until you showed me this..."

She gestured at the doorway. "That's unnerving."

"Want to go through? Visit my lab?"

She shook her head and crossed her arms. "Are you kidding?"

"No. It's perfectly safe, trust me." Auggy took three steps that carried him through the interface back into the cooler lab. Turning to face her, he saw Cicy's eyes widen as the cat sat up on the couch. Marie gapped at him.

The visibility setting allowed sound to travel across the interface. "Marie, it's fine. Come on, let me show you what I've been working on." He held his hand out across the interface.

Marie took a deep breath. She slid her phone into her pocket. She pushed her fists down next to her hips. Then she strode forward. She didn't take his hand, brushing past it, to step through the interface. He pulled his arm back as she stepped into the lab.

She gasped, looking around with wide eyes, until she turned back around and saw her apartment through the open doorway.

"Oh, shit. Shit, Auggy!" She turned on him, surprising him. Her hands hit at his chest, flat palms, not too hard. "Shit! Auggy, how did you do this?"

He caught her small wrists. "Come on, let me show you."

AFTER SHOWING Marie around the lab and demonstrating a few of the doorway interface configurations, she held up her hands. "Stop. Auggy, just stop for a second."

He tried to keep his face blank to hide his nervousness. He didn't know what she was going to say. He wanted to sit down, but right then he couldn't move. He watched her instead as she seemed to be thinking.

Finally, she took a breath and said, "You came up with a unified theory of everything—and used it to create this?"

He nodded.

"This started when you were working all the time, canceling dates, not responding to my calls or texts?"

The feeling of pride that had started rising immediately subsided. Her tone made it clear—she wasn't happy. She wasn't congratulating him on his discoveries or inventions.

"Yes, I'm sorry. I got so focused, I couldn't think about anything else."

She crossed her arms. "Obviously. You disappeared. I get it. You've always had that obsessive streak when you're fixated on something. It was alarming when *I* was the target. Why are you showing me this now?"

"I need your help figuring out what to do."

"That's obvious. Why did you do all these stupid pranks with Mars? What was that supposed to accomplish?"

Auggy felt his neck reddening. "I don't know. We've got enough problems here. I got the idea, it sounded funny. Then everyone thought it was a hoax, and—"

"You had to prove it wasn't."

"I suppose."

Marie closed the distance between them until she was within arms reach.

She looked up into his eyes. "It was really fucking stupid, Auggy. Like, destabilizing governments, stupid. You announced to the world that *someone* has that kind of power. *It's scary, Auggy. Terrifying.* If I wasn't standing here right now, I wouldn't believe it. Someone with that kind of power could do unthinkable things."

"That's why I need you," Auggy said. "You have a lot more common sense. I need a partner to figure this all out."

She cocked her head to the left, squinting slightly as she studied his face. "A partner with better sense? Clearly. That doesn't mean it has to be *me*. What else are you expecting?"

"I want to make up for hurting you. I want us back together. It's overwhelming, but I can deal with it, if you're with me."

"You realize I have my own plans, right? I have research that I'm trying to do. Things that I want to study, mister theory of everything. Am I supposed to give that all up?"

Auggy *knew* he was fucking up. He

shook his head. "That's not what I meant. At all." He gestured at the doorway. "With this—we can get views from *anywhere*. What would you think if I put a telescope in space fourteen billion lightyears away?"

She said evenly, "You can't do that."

"Not yet, no," he said. "Not with what I have here. Distance is a factor along with the energy requirements. But that's something that we can scale. The power generators use the inflation of the universe—and the ones I've built so far can power the doorway to any location within a thousand lightyears."

He saw the doubt, the curiosity, on her face. *She's tempted.* He quickly moved over to his chair and sat down, picking up a tablet. He pulled up a menu of shortcuts he had already made. He spun the chair and pointed at the platform. The doorway remained, showing her apartment. Cicy had gotten up from the couch and had walked closer, lifting her head and peering through the doorway.

Auggy tapped the first bookmark.

Marie's apartment vanished. Instead the doorway showed a dusty, gray, cratered landscape with low hills and the ungainly shape of the Apollo 17 lander.

"That's the Moon!" She said, then, "Isn't that the picture you have in your fake pod thing in the basement?"

"It is—except that's *actually* an interface like this one behind the window, set to show this spot. This is live, real-time, our own private view of the Moon."

He touched another bookmark.

Another barren, rocky landscape, except dimmer and reddish in hue. The shadows stretched out from a rocky cliff that rose up into the sky unbelievably high, turning hazy before the top. Marie uncrossed her arms and took a step closer to the platform, transfixed by the view.

"Is that Mars?"

"Valles Marineris—a few from the bottom, looking up at the cliff."

He'd saved the best for last. The discovery that would convince her, he was sure. He touched the bookmark.

Darkness filled the doorway, except

there was a sense of movement. Marie looked at him, eyebrows rising. Auggy grinned and touched the control to turn out the lights around the platform, leaving only dim illumination around the edges of the room. As his eyes adapted to the darkness, lights flowered into view through the doorway. A whole universe of complex light in blues, greens, reds, and yellows that pulsed and spiraled as they moved in the dark beyond the doorway. It all happened with a slow motion feel. From tiny sparkles of gold and red, to large spiral red conical patterns, to long ribbons that ripples as they moved across the view.

Marie caught his arm. Despite the shadows, he could make out the wonder and excitement on her face. "What is it?"

"Europa."

She kept staring for several seconds. Then she looked down at him and back at the view. "Europa?"

"Yep. One of the first places I looked with the doorway. I had to know."

"Those are living things—on Europa." She laughed and pressed her hands together in front of her mouth. "That's, that's..."

Her grip tightened on his arm. "Don't change it, Auggy. I want to see."

# CHAPTER 9

# UNIFIED SECRETS, INC.

A WIDE VISTA stretched in front of the curved window at the front of the building. Currently it showed a gasses pulled off a blue-white star spiraling into the accretion disk of a black hole over ten thousand light years away. The interface didn't allow any of the harmful radiation to pass—only a tolerably intense visible light spectrum. It illuminated the room with the unearthly glow, throwing Marie into (*a very nice*) silhouette. Auggy held two coffee cups as he crossed the room to join her. He passed her sweet mocha latte over.

"Here you go."

She took it, smiling, and leaned slightly closer so her shoulder brushed his arm. "I wish we could share this—I know so many people who would give anything for this view."

He slid his free arm around her waist. "You set the rules."

"I know. It's for the best. Right now. I still see conspiracy theories about the Mars missions. People can't deny that the missions are back exactly where they were, nothing changed. The rumors that it was a prank, a hack in the communications, with extremely realistic duplicates put at the space centers —many people accept it, because the alternative is unbelievable."

Auggy laughed. "It was pretty funny."

She shook her head. "Only you would think so. No more pranks."

"No more pranks," he said. "The media is having a field day with the latest dossier. I don't think Senator Simmons will remain in office much longer. It has everyone in D.C. running scared."

"It should," Marie said. "All their dirty little secrets flushed out into the open. People can elect honest politicians for once."

"I didn't expect the doorway to become a political tool."

"The world has to change."

"The world has to change," he said, echoing her. "You're right. I agree. That's why I asked for your help."

"And we get to use it for our own research," she said, sipping her coffee as she gazed out at a view no other humans had ever seen.

Auggy knew she was right about it all. Their new company (*with their intelligence gathering and resources*) was investing in all sorts of solutions to problems. And in most cases, those resulted in a profitable outcome for the company itself. Only their most trusted partners even knew of the doorway's existence. That number would grow, he knew, but they had a long time together to figure it all out.

He hugged her close and looked out at the black hole. He said, "I'm so attracted to you right now."

Marie laughed and gave him a shove. "That's terrible."

He kissed the top of her head.

———

Ryan M. Williams is a full-time career librarian and a multi-genre writer with over twenty books. He writes across a range of genres including science fiction, fantasy, paranormal, mystery, horror, and romance. He earned a Master of Arts degree in writing popular fiction from Seton Hill University and a Master of Library and Information Science from San Jose University. His short fiction has appeared in Pulphouse Fiction Magazine, On Spec Magazine, and anthologies from Pocket Books and WMG Publishing.

# POEVILLE

The POEVILLE series with feline detective C. Auguste Dupin and his human librarian Penny Copper might be just the thing.

•The Murders in the Reed Moore Library

•The Task of Auntie Dido

## MOREAU SOCIETY

Brock Marsden, a genetically-modified detective, solves the toughest cases in a this far future space opera series.

•Dark Matters

•The Gingerbread House

•Past Lives

•Past Dark

# DEAD THINGS

Do you like your fantasy dark and paranormal? Ravyn Washington isn't like other students. Her grandmother was called a witch and if the Inquisition discovers

Ravyn's abilities she could burn in the DEAD THINGS series.

•Waking Dead Things

•Dreaming Dead Things

•Killing Dead Things

## FILMING DEAD THINGS

Filming the Inquisition at work made Stefan Roland's ground-breaking documentary directing career—calling him the Jane Goodall of Dead Things.

•Farm of the Dead Things

•Mall of the Dead Things

•War of the Dead Things

•Trailer Park of the Dead Things

## SCIENCE FICTION STORIES & NOVELS

Discover more science fiction with these books.

•Infestation

•Europan Holiday

•Stowaway to Eternity

•Crunch Bang: The Chrystal Eagle Stories

•Space Monkeys: A Short Science Fiction First Contact Story

•Invasion of the Book Snatchers: A Short Science Fiction Story of Small-Town Terror

## ROMANCE BY KATE N. RYAN

And if you like romance and comedy, the books by KATE N. RYAN will tickle your funny bone—and more.

•Watching You Sleep: a laugh out loud romantic comedy

•Tom Scratch: A Short Fantastic Romance Story

www.ingramcontent.com/pod-product-compliance
Lightning Source LLC
Chambersburg PA
CBHW030907200726

48289CB00003B/933